TRUE STORY

To Rachel

Cats rule

MARTY CHAN   ILLUSTRATED BY LORNA BENNETT

True Story

Ink Jockey Incorporated
10539 – 75 Street
Edmonton, Alberta, Canada
T6A 2Z6

Library and Archives Canada
Cataloguing in Publication

Chan, Marty
True story / written by Marty Chan;
illustrated by Lorna Bennett.

ISBN 978-0-9810449-0-3
I. Bennett, Lorna, 1960- II. Title.
PS8555.H39244T78 2009   jC813'.54   C2008-907624-9

Cover and Book Design
Perry Shulak / Critical Fusion

Printed and bound in Canada

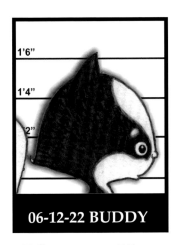

1'6"
1'4"
2"

06-12-22 BUDDY

For Edmonton Humane
Society – M.C.

1'6"
1'
1'2
1'

06-07-15 MAX

For Cherie Hall – L.B.

Don't let his big bright eyes fool you.
My cat is a troublemaker.

He scribbled on the wall with crayons.

He made Swiss cheese out of my shirts,
and he crashed my race car.

Max messed up my room.
True story.

Don't let his sweet kitty breath fool you.
My cat is a stinker.

He got scared when I turned on the blender. He knocked over the garbage can.

And he let out a stress fart.

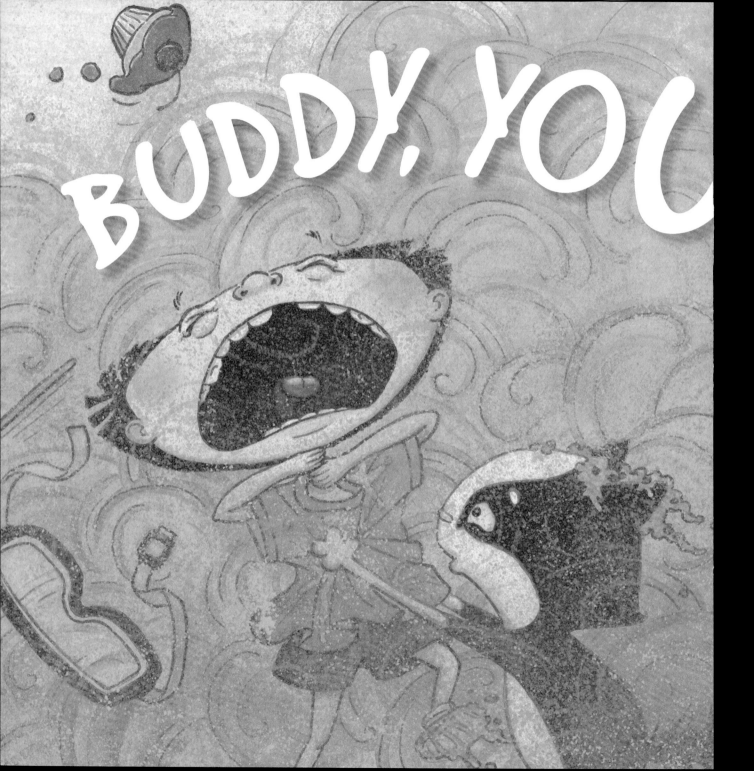

REEK!

Buddy stunk up the kitchen.
True story.

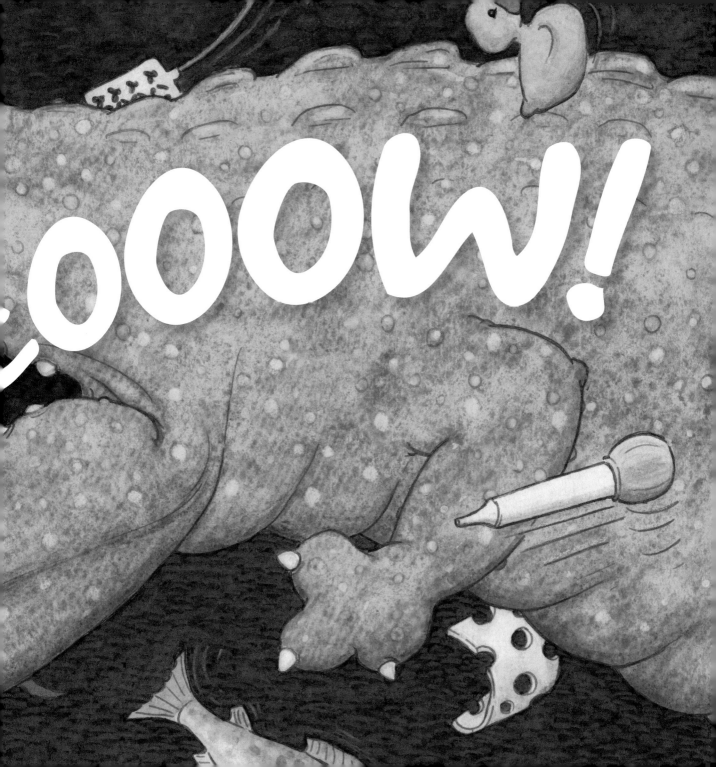

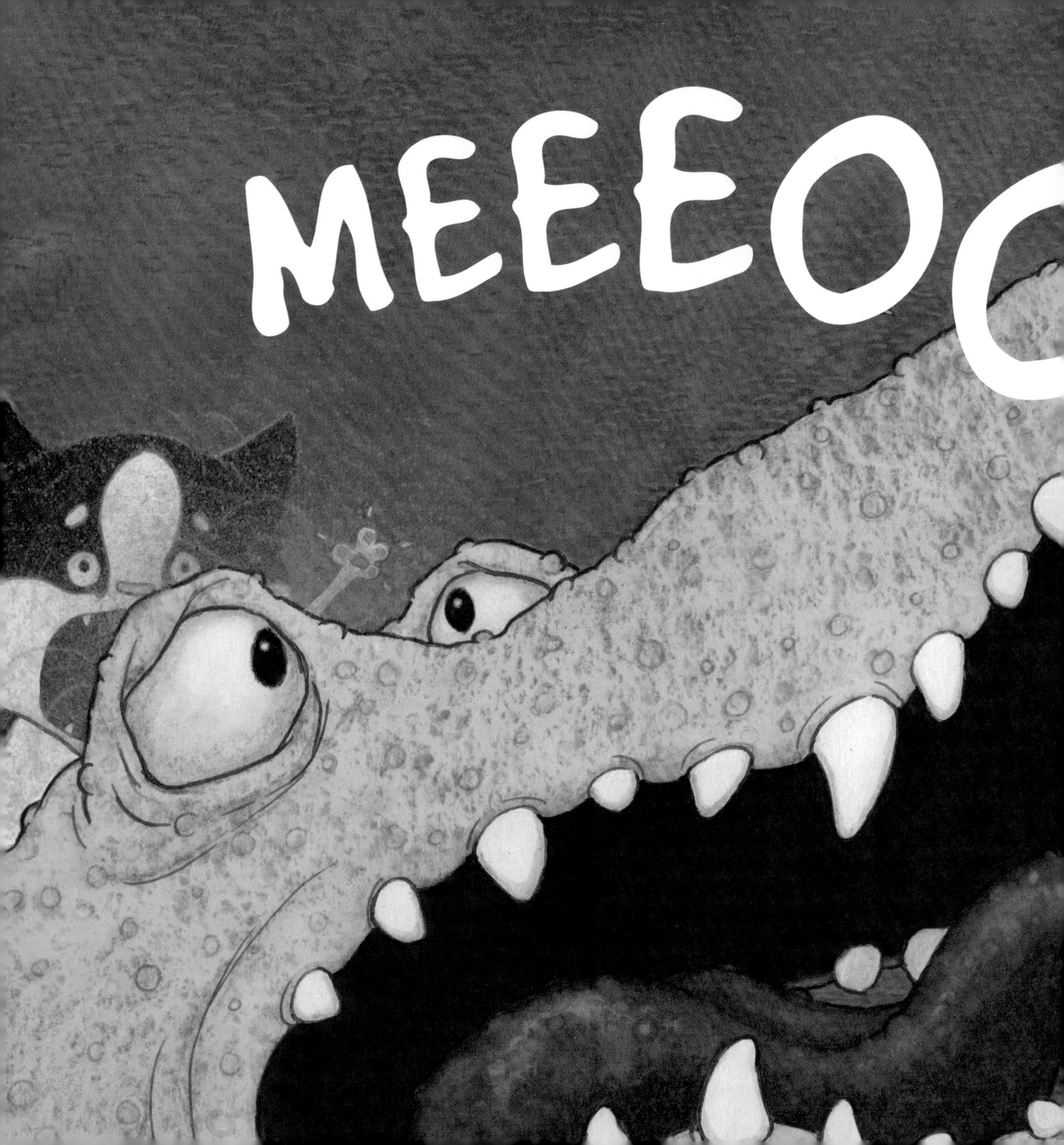
MEEEO

Max wrestled with Buddy's tail and scared the toot out of his brother.

They growled.

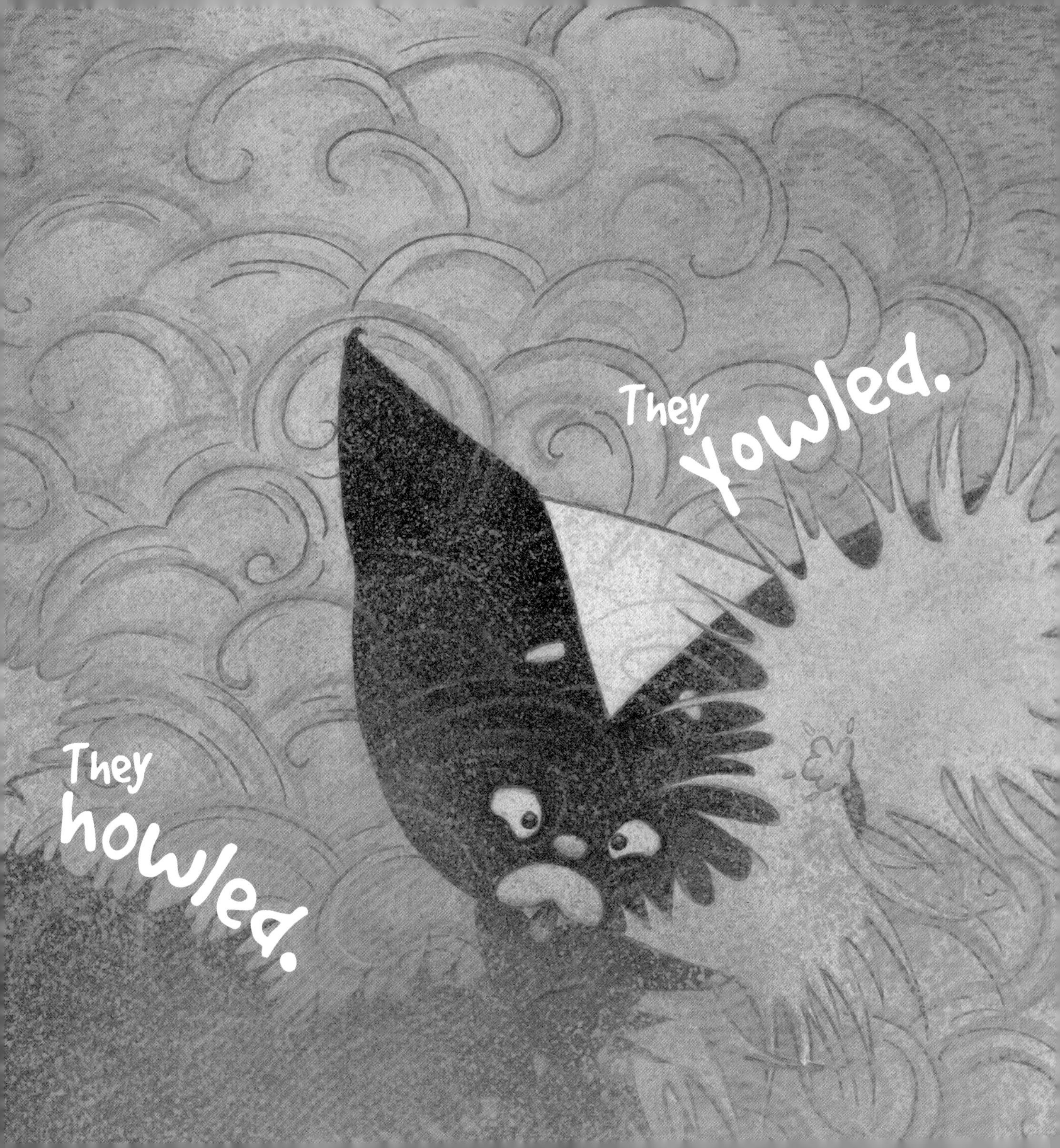

They howled.

They yowled.

Buddy needed a safe place to hide, and the safest place to hide was...

In my bedroom...

on my bed...